# SCOTT, FORESMAN FIRST TALKING STORYBOOK BOX

A is for Alphabet by Cathy, Marly, and Wendy

Anatole by Eve Titus

Angelo the Naughty One by Helen Garrett

Benjie by Joan M. Lexau

Chicken Licken

Frances Face-Maker by William Cole

Harry the Dirty Dog by Gene Zion

Humbug Witch by Lorna Balian

Jack and the Beanstalk

Little Bear's Pancake Party by Janice

Mickey's Magnet by Franklyn M. Branley and Eleanor K. Vaughan

Mother Goose Rhymes

Over in the Meadow by John Langstaff

Straight Up by Henry B. Lent

The House That Jack Built

The Little Rabbit Who Wanted Red Wings by Carolyn Sherwin Bailey

The Shoemaker and the Elves

The Tale of the Flopsy Bunnies by Beatrix Potter

Timothy Turtle by Al Graham

What Mary Jo Shared by Janis Udry

Where's Andy? by Jane Thayer

# HUMBUG WITCH

## Lorna Balian

ABINGDON

NEW YORK                    NASHVILLE

Special Scott, Foresman and Company Edition
for *Scott, Foresman First Talking Storybook Box*

This special edition is printed and distributed by Scott, Foresman and Company
by special arrangement with Abingdon Press, 201 Eighth Avenue South,
Nashville, Tennessee, 37203.

For Jennifer,

Jill,

Kate,

Daniel,

and

John

# There was this Witch . . .

And all of her was little

Except her nose.
That was very **BIG.**
She had two crooked teeth
And long, stringy, red hair.

It was so long she kept tripping over it.

She wore a slightly squashed,

tall,

black,

pointed hat

like Witches always wear,

Orange gloves,
A handknit black wool shawl,
An old plaid apron,
Red and white striped stockings,
And funny looking black shoes
With gold buckles on them.

She had a good sturdy broom,
And a black cat
Named Fred.

# You can see for yourself . . .

She was truly a frightening looking,

Horrible,

Witchey,

## WITCH!

# But . . .

When she tried to *do* things
They never worked the way they were supposed to
For Witches.

Like
When she wanted to laugh wickedly and scare everyone.
It never sounded "Cackle-Cackle-Cackle."
It always sounded "Giggle-Giggle-Giggle."

Or like
When she wanted to go to Portugal,
Or Chicago,
Or to the next-door neighbors,
She would climb on her good sturdy broom
And say all sorts of magic words,
And wait a few minutes . . .


And NOTHING would happen.


Then she would jiggle her good sturdy broom
And say more magic words,
Real LOUD
And wait a l-o-n-g time . . .
And still
Nothing would happen.
Nothing at all!

The broom would not move an inch.

When she wanted to turn Fred into an alligator,
Or a hippopotamus,
Or a candy bar,
She would get down on her hands and knees
And look Fred square in the eye
And say all kinds of magic words,

And wait . . .

And wait . . .

But Fred just stayed a cat!

When she wanted to cook up a batch of Magic Potion,
She would dump all the very best things
In her very best kettle . . .
Things like


SOUR MILK
PAPRIKA
MOLASSES
PRUNE PITS
EGG SHELLS
HAIR TONIC
APPLE PEELINGS
PICKLE JUICE
CINNAMON
GENUINE RAINWATER
COUGH SYRUP

And

*Peanut Butter.*

And she would stir it
And stir it
And stir it.
And say all the magic words she could think of.
And then she would stir it some more.

It sizzled a little,
But it never got smoky,
Or bubbly,
Or EXPLODED

Like Magic Potions are supposed to do.

All it did was make Fred terribly sick
To his stomach!

She finally decided it was just no use!
She stood her good sturdy broom in the corner.

She took off her funny looking black shoes
With the gold buckles.

She took off her plaid apron.

She took off her handknit black wool shawl.

She took off her slightly squashed,

Tall,

Black,

Pointed hat.

She took off her orange gloves.

And she took off her long, stringy, red hair.

She took off her *mask.*

And went to bed.

So did Fred.